Horrorgami

SPOOKY PAPER FOLDING FOR CHILDREN

STEVE AND MEGUMI BIDDLE
Illustrations by Megumi Biddle

RANDOM HOUSE

ABOUT THE AUTHORS

Steve Biddle is a professional entertainer with a speciality act that has taken him all over the world. He studied origami in Japan with the top Japanese origami masters, thereby acquiring deeper knowledge of a subject that has always fascinated him. Megumi Biddle is a highly qualified graphic artist, designer and illustrator, with a long-standing interest in paper and its many applications.

Steve and Megumi combine their talents to design items for television, feature films and major advertising campaigns, and in writing books for children and adults.

They have taken their craft all over the country to schools, festivals and arts centres and currently present a weekly origami programme for Sky TV.

A Random House Book Published by Random House Children's Books 20 Vauxhall Bridge Road, London SW1V 2SA A division of Random House UK Ltd London Melbourne Sydney Auckland Johannesburg and agencies throughout the world Text © Steve and Megumi Biddle 1996 Illustrations © Megumi Biddle 1996 1 3 5 7 9 10 8 6 4 2 First published in Great Britain by Random House 1996 This book is sold subject to the condition that it shall not, by way of trade or otherwise, be lent, resold, hired out, or otherwise circulated without the publisher's prior consent in any form of binding or cover other than that in which it is published and without a similar condition including this condition being imposed on the subsequent purchaser. The right of Steve and Megumi Biddle to be identified as the authors and illustrator of this work has been asserted by them in accordance with the Copyright, Designs and Patents Act, 1988. Printed and bound in Hong Kong Random House UK Limited Reg. No. 954009. ISBN 0099601613

INTRODUCTION

Do you like to be scared silly? Do you like it even better when you're the one who's doing the scaring? Either way, turn the pages of this book very carefully - it's full of monstrously simple things to fold. There's a gruesome spider hanging about, and beware of the creepy witch - she might change you into a rat!

Horrorgami features traditional origami folds as well as many new ones, which you'll enjoy whether you're an experienced paper folder or have never tried origami before. To get the most out of this book, you will probably find it easiest to work your way through from beginning to end, as many of the folds and folding procedures are based on previous ones.

All of the origami projects in this book start with one or more squares of paper. Packets of origami paper, coloured on one side and white on the other, can be bought from department stores, toy shops, stationery shops and oriental gift shops. Why not try using the fancy gift-wrapping papers that are now widely available? You could even cut out a few pages from a colour magazine!

To help you become accomplished at paper folding, here are some tips:

- Fold on a flat surface, such as a table or book.
- Make your folds and cuts neat and accurate.
- Crease your folds into place by running your thumbnail along them.
- In the illustrations, the shading represents the coloured side of the paper.
- Try to get hold of the right kind of paper to match the origami that you plan to fold. This will improve the finished result.
- Before you start, make sure your paper is square.
- Above all, if a fold or a whole model does not work out, don't give up. Put the fold to one side and come back to it another day.

If you want to learn more about origami, contact the British Origami Society, 35 Corte Crescent, Hazelgrove, Stockport, Cheshire, SK7 5PR.

In the United States, contact Origami USA, 15 West 77th Street, New York, NY 10024-5192.

We would very much like to hear from you about your interest in origami, or if you have any problems obtaining origami materials. So please do write to us, care of our publishers, enclosing a stamped addressed envelope.

Remember that the real secret of origami lies in the giving and sharing with others. We do hope that you have a lot of fun and enjoyment with **Horrorgami**.

Steve and Megumi

Acknowledgements
We would like to thank Mikael Kristensen (a spider fanatic) and Mark Axton for their help and support with Horrorgami.

CONTENTS

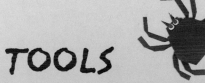

TOOLS

More often than not all that you require for making many of the **Horrorgami** projects is a tube of stick glue, pencil, scissors, ruler, felt-tip pens. Always take great care when handling the scissors. It is a good idea to keep all your tools in a safe place, out of the reach of small children.

BLOOD DROP

This model will add a touch of the macabre to any Halloween invite.

You will need:
Square of paper, coloured on one side and white on the other

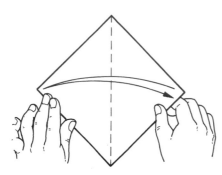

1 Turn the square around to look like a diamond, with the white side on top. Fold and unfold it in half from side to side.

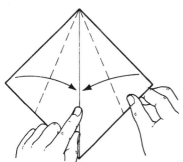

2 From the top point, fold the sloping sides in to meet the middle fold-line, so making a shape that in origami is called the kite base.

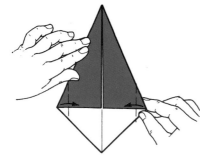

3 Fold a little of each side point over.

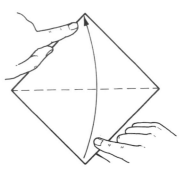

4 Fold a little of the bottom point up.

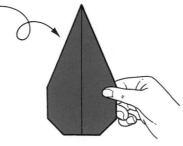

5 To complete the blood drop, turn it over from side to side.

WIZARD'S HAT

When carefully folded out of colourful paper, this model makes a perfect gift tag or decoration.

You will need:
Square of paper, coloured on one side and white on the other

1 Turn the square around to look like a diamond, with the white side on top. Fold it in half from bottom to top, so making a shape that in origami is called the diaper fold.

4

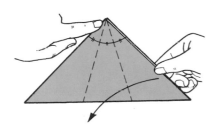

2 From the top point, fold the right-hand sloping side over to a point one-third of the way across the diaper fold.

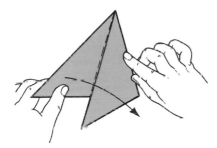

3 From the top point, fold the left-hand sloping side over so that it lies on top.

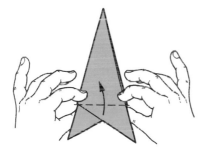

4 Fold the bottom points up as shown.

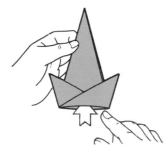

5 To complete the wizard's hat, open it out along the bottom edge.

WEREWOLF CLAW

Creep up on your friends and terrify them with this hideous claw.

You will need:
7cm square of paper, coloured on one side and white on the other

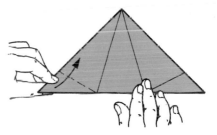

2 Along the existing fold-line, fold the left-hand point over as shown.

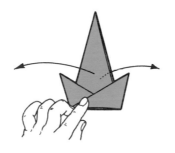

1 Repeat steps 1 to 4 of the WIZARD's HAT on page 4. Unfold the paper, back to the diaper fold.

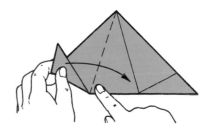

3 Along the existing fold-line, fold the left-hand sloping side over.

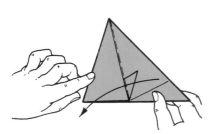

4 Repeat step 3 with the right-hand sloping side, so that it lies on top.

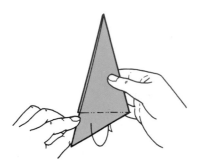

5 Along the existing fold-line, tuck the bottom point up inside the model.

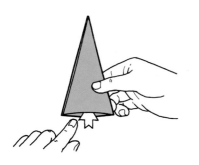

6 To complete the werewolf claw, open it out along the bottom edge.

CANDLE AND CANDLESTICK

This model will light up any spooky Halloween event. It will also work well at Christmas time too.

You will need:
3 squares of paper all the same size, coloured on one side and white on the other
Scissors
Glue

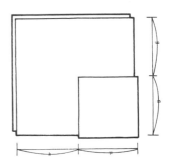

1 **Flame:** From one square, cut out a square for the flame to the size shown.

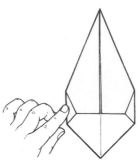

2 Repeat steps 1 to 3 of the BLOOD DROP on page 4.

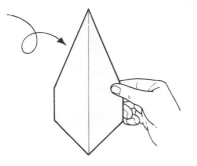

3 To complete the flame, turn it over from side to side.

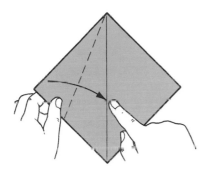

4 Candle: With another square, repeat step 1 of the BLOOD DROP on page 4, but with the coloured side on top. From the top point, fold the left-hand sloping side in to meet the middle fold-line.

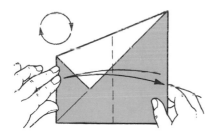

5 Turn the paper around into the position shown. Fold and unfold it in half from side to side.

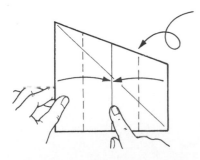

6 Turn the paper over. Fold the sides in to meet the middle fold-line.

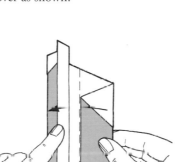

7 Fold the left-hand middle edge over as shown.

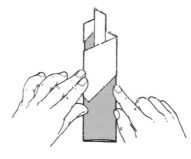

8 Fold the paper in half from right to left.

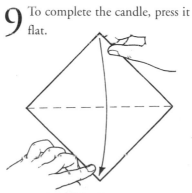

9 To complete the candle, press it flat.

10 Candlestick: Turn the remaining square around to look like a diamond, with the white side on top. Fold it in half from top to bottom, so making an upside-down diaper fold.

11 Fold and unfold the diaper fold in half from side to side.

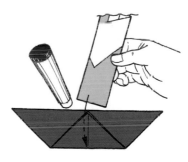

12 To complete the candlestick, fold its bottom points up to meet the top edge.

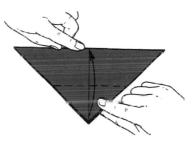

13 Assembly: Glue the candle behind the points.

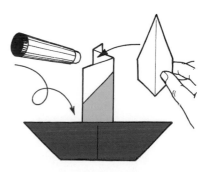

14 To complete the candle and candlestick, turn the model over and glue the flame on to the candle.

MAN IN THE MOON

This model is perfect for any night-time origami scene.

You will need:
Square of paper, coloured on one side and white on the other

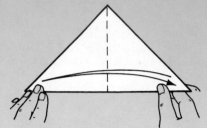

1 Repeat step 1 of the WIZARD'S HAT on page 4. Fold and unfold the diaper fold in half from side to side.

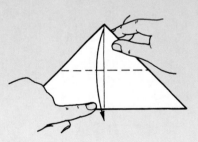

2 Fold the top points down together, so that they overlap the bottom edge.

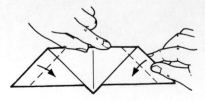

3 Fold the right and left-hand sloping sides over as shown.

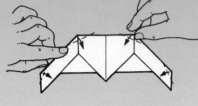

4 Fold a little of the side points over.

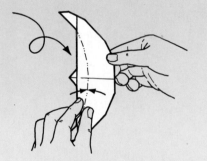

5 Turn the paper over and around into the position shown. Press the Man in the Moon's face into shape.

6 Here is the completed Man in the Moon. You can stick on a paper eye for extra effect.

FOX

Here, from just three simple shapes, you can make a howling fox that is likely to scare just about anyone.

You will need:

3 squares of paper all the same size, coloured on one side and white on the other
Felt-tip pen
Glue

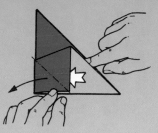

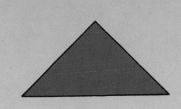

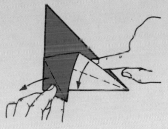

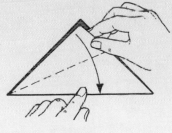

1 **Body:** Repeat step 1 of the WIZARD'S HAT on page 4, with one square.

2 **Tail:** Repeat steps 10 to 12 of the CANDLESTICK on page 7, with another square.

3 **Face:** Repeat step 1 of the WIZARD'S HAT on page 4, with the remaining square, but with the coloured side on top. From the left-hand point, fold the topmost sloping side down to meet the bottom edge.

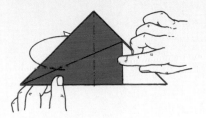

4 Fold the left-hand point behind to the right-hand point.

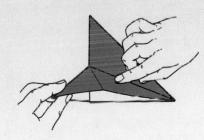

5 Pull the top flap of paper over...

6 to the left, so its sloping side meets the bottom edge. Press the paper flat to...

7 make a triangular point.

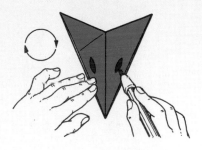

8 Turn the paper around into the position shown. To complete the fox's face, draw on its eyes with the felt-tip pen.

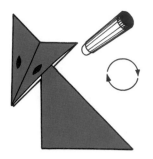

9 **Assembly:** Turn the body around into the position shown and glue it to the inside of the fox's face.

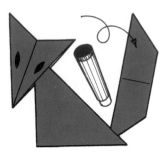

10 To complete the fox, turn the tail over and glue it on to the fox's body as shown.

TWINKLING STAR

Here is a very simple way to make a star. It will look most beautiful when made out of shining metallic foil (the kind that is used for gift-wrapping).

You will need:

2 squares of paper the same size, coloured on one side and white on the other
Glue

1 **Square A:** Repeat steps 3 to 7 of the FOX on page 9, with one square.

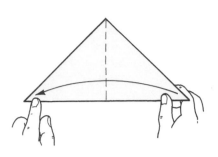

2 **Square B:** Repeat step 1 of the WIZARD'S HAT on page 4, with the remaining square. Fold the diaper fold in half from right to left, so...

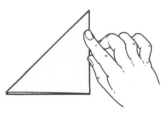

3 making a triangle. Press it flat.

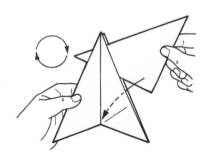

4 **Assembly:** Turn parts A and B around into the positions shown. Tuck part B inside part A.

5 To complete the twinkling star, glue both parts together.

HALLOWEEN CAT

As Halloween approaches, you may want to decorate your home in the ghostly spirit of the season, whether you are having a party or not.

You will need:
2 squares of paper the same size, coloured on one side and white on the other
Felt-tip pen
Glue

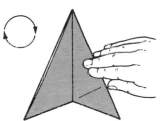

1 **Body:** Repeat steps 3 to 7 of the FOX on page 9, with one square. Turn the paper around into the position shown.

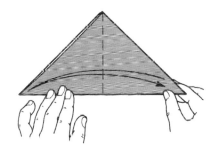

2 **Face:** Repeat step 1 of the WIZARD's HAT on page 4, with the remaining square.

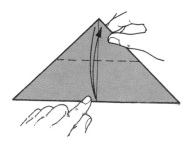

3 Fold and unfold the diaper fold in half from top to bottom.

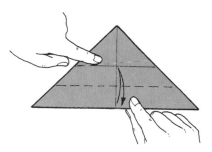

4 Fold the bottom edge up to meet the fold-line made in step 3. Press it flat and unfold it.

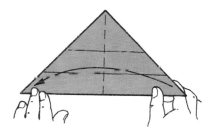

5 Fold the diaper fold in half from right to left, so making a triangle.

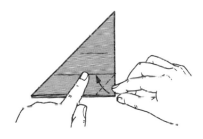

6 Fold the bottom right-hand point up to meet the fold-line made in step 4.

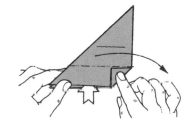

7 Insert a finger underneath the triangle's top layer. Open it out and...

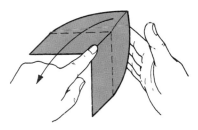

8 with your free hand, press the triangle's top point...

9 down neatly as shown.

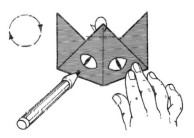
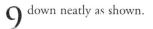

10 Turn the paper around into the position shown. Fold a little of the top points behind. To complete the cat's face, draw on its eyes with the felt-tip pen.

11 **Assembly:** Glue the cat's head on to its body as shown. To complete the Halloween cat, fold a little of its bottom points over, so suggesting paws.

GOBLIN'S HAT

Here is another way to make a hat. If made from a sheet of wrapping paper, it will become a great hat to wear when you go trick-or-treating.

You will need:
Square of paper, coloured on one side and white on the other
Felt-tip pen

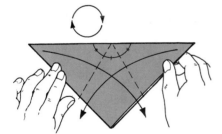

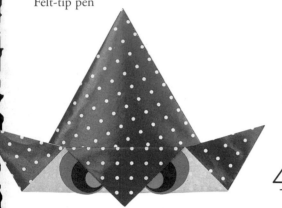

1 Repeat step 1 of the WIZARD'S HAT on page 4. Turn the diaper fold around so that it points towards you. Fold the right- and left-hand halves of the top edge over as shown.

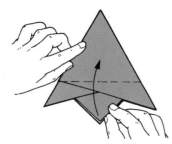

2 Fold the two side points and the topmost bottom point up as shown.

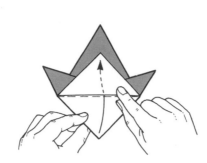

3 Tuck the remaining bottom point up inside the model.

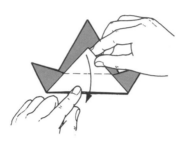

4 Fold the point down as shown, so that it overlaps the bottom edge.

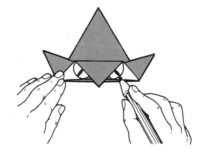

5 Using the felt-tip pen, draw on the goblin's eyes. To complete the goblin's hat, open it out along the bottom edge.

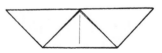

JACK-O'-LANTERN

A grinning jack-o'-lantern is the universal symbol of Halloween, but did you know that turnips instead of pumpkins were originally used?

You will need:
2 squares of paper the same size, coloured on one side and white on the other
Scissors
Glue

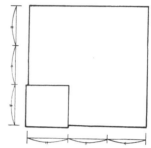

1 **Mouth:** From one square, cut out a square for the mouth to the size shown.

2 To complete the mouth, repeat steps 10 to 12 of the CANDLESTICK on page 7.

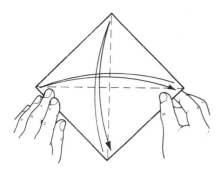

3 **Lantern:** With the white side on top, fold and unfold the remaining square's opposite corners together in turn to mark the diagonal fold lines, then open up again.

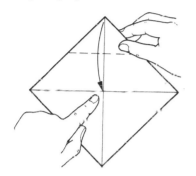

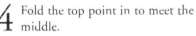

4 Fold the top point in to meet the middle.

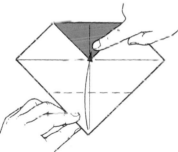

5 Fold the bottom point up, so that it overlaps the middle.

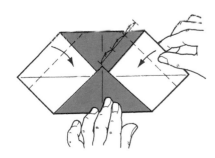

6 Fold the top right- and left-hand sloping sides over as far as shown.

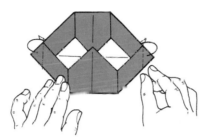

7 Fold the bottom right- and left-hand sloping sides over as far as shown.

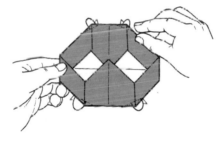

8 Fold the two side points behind.

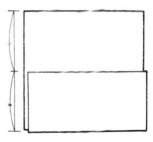

9 Shape the lantern by folding its top and bottom points behind.

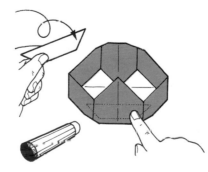

10 To complete the jack-o'-lantern, turn the mouth over and glue it on the lantern, as shown by the dotted lines.

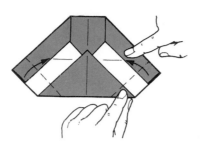

GRUESOME SKULL

Take particular care to fold this origami model accurately for the neatest possible result.

You will need:
2 squares of paper the same size, coloured on one side and white on the other
Scissors
Glue

1 **Teeth:** From one square, cut out a rectangle for the teeth to the size shown.

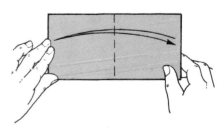

2 Place the rectangle sideways on, with the coloured side on top. Fold and unfold it in half from side to side.

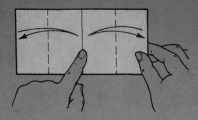

3 Fold the sides in to meet the middle fold-line. Press them flat and unfold them.

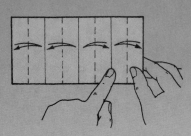

4 Divide the length in to eight equal sections by folding. Press the folds flat and unfold them.

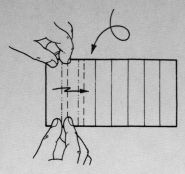

5 Turn the paper over. From one end pleat the paper as shown.

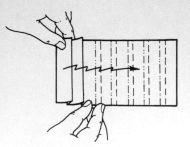

6 Take great care with the pleating, and make sure your folding is neat and tidy.

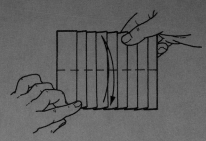

7 Fold and unfold the paper in half from bottom to top.

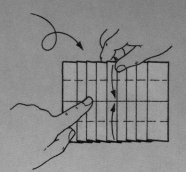

8 Fold the top and bottom edges in to meet the middle fold-line.

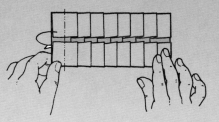

9 Fold the left-hand side behind as shown.

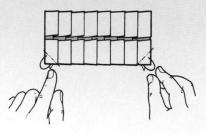

10 To complete the teeth, fold their bottom right- and left-hand points behind.

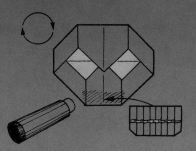

11 **Head:** Repeat steps 3 to 8 of the JACK-O'-LANTERN on page 13, with the remaining square, but with the coloured side on top. Turn the paper around into the position shown. Glue the teeth on to the head, as shown by the shaded part.

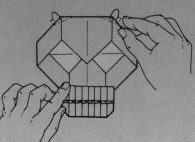

12 To complete the gruesome skull, fold a little of its top points behind.

PHANTOM OF THE OPERA

To make this phantom extra-frightening, illuminate from below with a torch.

You will need:
2 squares of paper the same size, coloured on one side and white on the other
Scissors
Glue

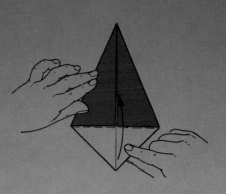

1 **Phantom's head:** From one square, cut out two squares for the head to the size shown.

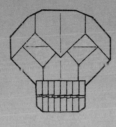

2 To complete the head, repeat steps 1 to 12 of the GRUESOME SKULL on pages 13 to 14.

3 **Phantom's body:** Repeat steps 1 and 2 of the BLOOD DROP on page 4 with the remaining square. Fold the bottom point up along the base of the large triangle.

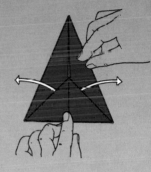

4 Unfold the sloping sides.

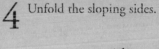

5 Fold the top point down as far as shown. Press it flat and unfold it.

6 Turn the paper over. Along the fold-line made in step 5, fold the top point down.

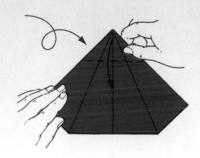

7 Fold the point back up, into the position shown by the dotted lines.

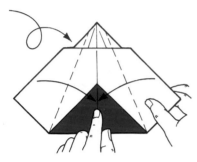

8 Turn the paper over. Along the existing fold-lines, fold the sloping sides over.

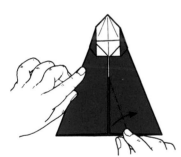

9 Fold the right-hand middle point over as shown.

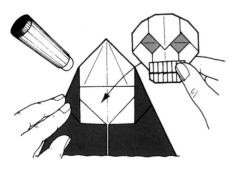

10 To complete the Phantom, glue its head on to the body as shown.

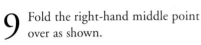

SPIDER AND THREAD

For a spooky effect, hang the spider somewhere that your Halloween guests might find themselves face to face with it.

You will need:
Square of paper, coloured on both sides
Scissors
Glue

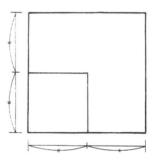

1 **Spider's body:** From the square, cut out a square for the body to the size shown. *Do not discard the remaining paper.*

2 Repeat steps 1 and 2 of the BLOOD DROP on page 4. Fold the kite base's top point down as far as shown.

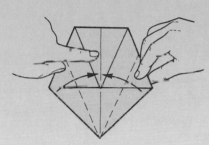

3 From the bottom point, fold the sloping sides in to meet the middle fold-line.

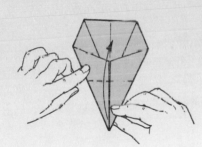

4 Fold the bottom point up and...

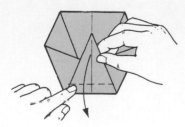

5 down, so making a small pleat.

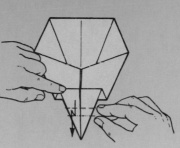

6 Repeat steps 4 and 5.

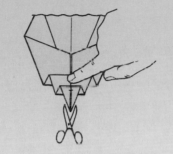

7 From the bottom point, cut along the middle fold-line as far as shown.

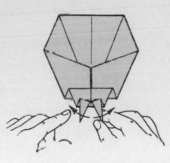

8 To complete the spider's body, spread the two bottom points apart.

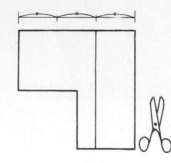

9 **Thread:** From the paper, cut out a rectangle for the thread to the size shown. *Do not discard the remaining paper.*

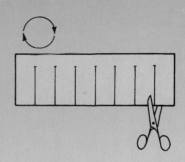

10 Place the rectangle sideways on. Now cut slits in the paper, first from the bottom edge and then...

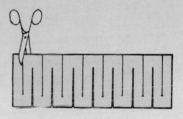

11 from the top edge. Be very careful *not* to cut right through to the opposite edges of the paper.

12 To complete the thread, carefully lift one end up, so as not to tear the paper.

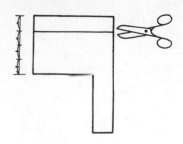

13 **Legs:** From the paper, cut out a rectangle for the legs to the size shown. You can now discard the remaining paper.

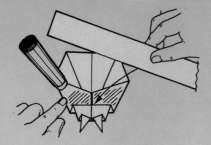

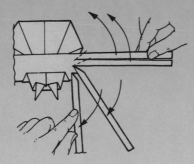

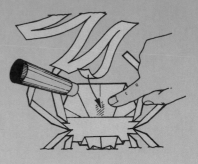

14 **Assembly:** Glue the rectangle on to the spider's body, as shown by the shaded part.

16 Fold the legs in to shape as shown.

18 Glue one end of the thread on to the spider's body, as shown by the shaded part.

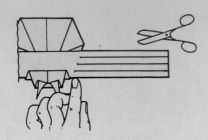

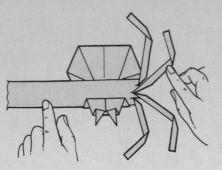

15 From one side of the rectangle, cut three slits in the paper, so making the spider's legs.

17 This should be the result. Repeat steps 15 and 16 on the other side of the rectangle.

19 To complete the spider, turn it over from side to side. The spider will wobble about when its thread is pulled up and down.

SPIDER'S WEB

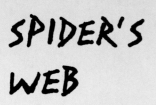

Make lots of webs to hang around your house or let your family and friends spin their own. This very simple fold is based on a paper-cutting technique called kirigami.

You will need:
Square of paper, coloured on one side and white on the other
Pencil
Scissors

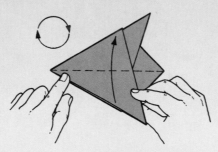

1 Repeat step 1 of the GOBLIN'S HAT on page 12. Turn the paper around into the position shown and fold it in half from bottom to top.

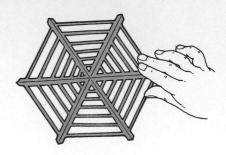

3 Carefully open out the paper to...

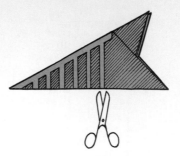

2 Using the pencil, copy this design on to the paper shape. Cut away and discard the shaded parts.

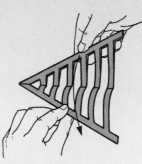

4 complete the spider's web.

CREEPY CATERPILLAR

This caterpillar will look extra-creepy if fluorescent paper is used to fold it.

You will need:
3 squares of paper all the same size, coloured on both sides
Scissors
Felt-tip pen
Glue

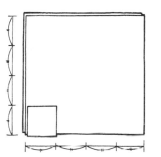

1 **Face:** From one square, cut out a square for the face to the size shown.

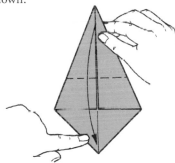

2 Repeat steps 1 and 2 of the BLOOD DROP on page 4. Fold the kite base's top point down and...

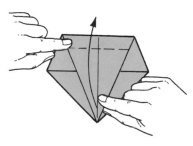

3 back up, so making...

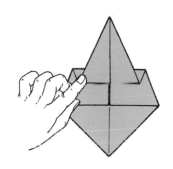

4 a pleat.

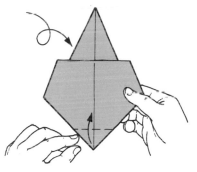

5 Turn the paper over. Fold a little of the bottom point up.

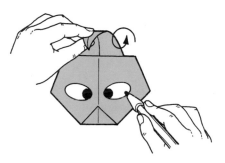

6 Curl the top point slightly. To complete the caterpillar's face, draw on its eyes with the felt-tip pen.

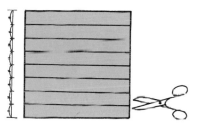

7 **Body:** From another square, cut eight equal rectangles of paper as shown.

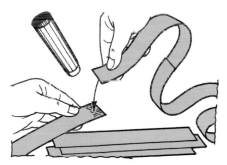

8 Glue the rectangles together, end to end, so making one long strip of paper. Repeat steps 7 and 8 with the remaining square.

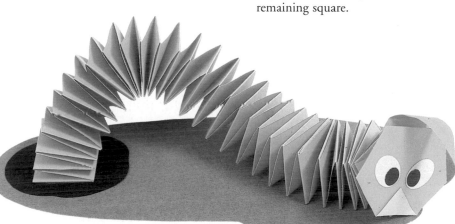

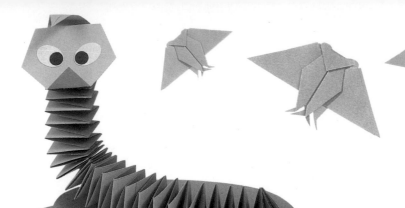

MONSTER MASK

By making slight variations in the folds you can easily create many different kinds of monsters.

You will need:
Square of paper, coloured on one side and white on the other

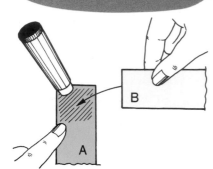

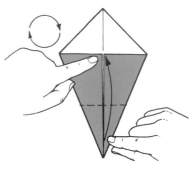

9 Using the felt-tip pen, label one strip A and the other B. Apply glue to the end of strip A. Lay strip B at right angles to strip A on to the glued area.

12 Fold strip A down over strip B.

1 Repeat steps 1 and 2 of the BLOOD DROP on page 4. Turn the kite base around into the position shown. Fold the bottom point up as far as shown, so making a triangle.

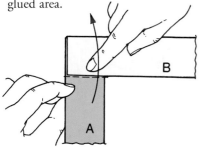

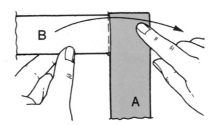

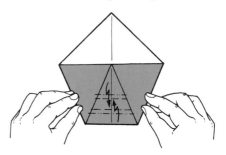

10 Fold strip A up and over strip B.

13 Fold strip B, across to the right, over strip A. Continue overlapping the strips until all of the paper is folded, so making a folded spring.

2 Pleat the triangle as shown, so making the monster's mouth and nose.

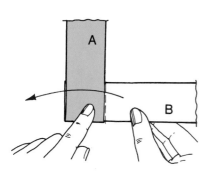

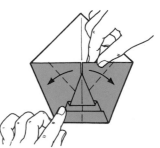

11 Fold strip B, across to the left, over strip A.

14 Apply glue to one end of the spring and attach it to the back of the caterpillar's face. To complete the creepy caterpillar, pull the spring out slightly.

3 Fold the two middle corners out, and...

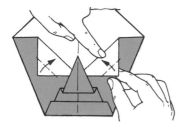

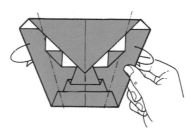

GHOST

Here's a good way to catch a ghost with origami, and if you're having a spooky get-together, you can write your invitations inside its folds.

You will need:
Square of paper, white on both sides
Felt-tip pen

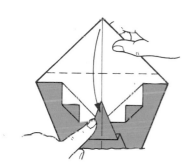

4 back over, so making the monster's eyes.

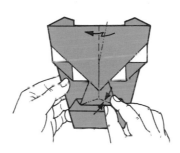

6 Shape the face by folding the sloping sides behind.

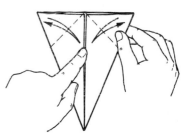

1 Repeat steps 1 and 2 of the BLOOD DROP on page 4. Turn the kite base around into the position shown. Fold the top point down and tuck it behind the front layers of paper.

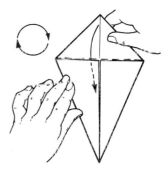

5 Fold the top point down as far as shown, so making the monster's forehead.

7 Pleat the monster's forehead and pinch its nose into shape.

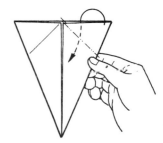

2 Fold the two top points down to meet the middle edges. Press them flat and unfold them.

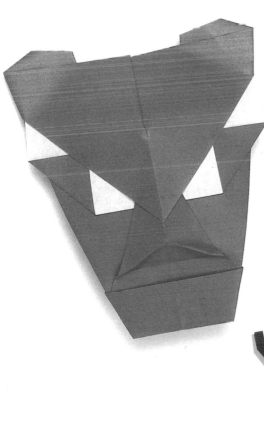

8 Here is the completed monster mask.

3 Now inside reverse fold the top right-hand point. This is what you do:

21

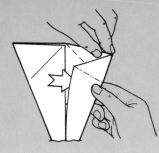

4 Using the fold-lines made in step 3 as a guide, push the right-hand point…

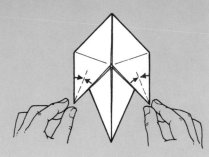

8 Pinch together each point's sloping sides and…

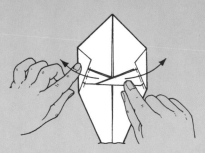

12 Fold the arms out to either side.

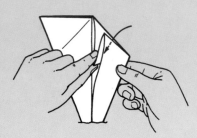

5 down inside the model as shown. Press the paper flat, so completing the reverse fold.

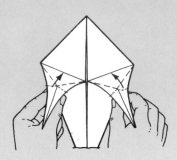

9 fold the small triangular flaps that appear…

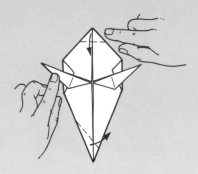

13 Fold the top point down and the bottom one across to the right.

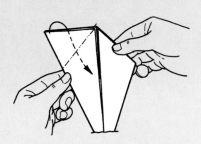

6 Repeat steps 3 to 5 with the top left-hand point.

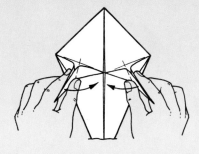

10 to one side and press them flat, so making the ghost's arms.

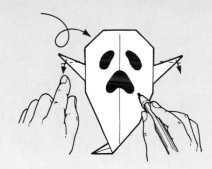

14 Turn the paper over. Shape the arms by folding their tips down. To complete the ghost, draw on its eyes and mouth with the felt-tip pen.

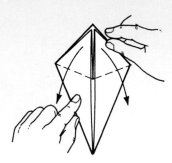

7 Fold the two top points down and out to either side as shown.

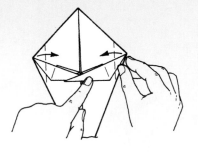

11 Fold a little of each side point over.

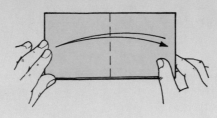

Hang your origami bats high up, where they can be mistaken for real vampire bats!

You will need:

Square of paper, coloured on one side and white on the other
Scissors

2 Fold and unfold in half from side to side.

3 Lift one half up along the middle fold-line. Start to open out the paper...

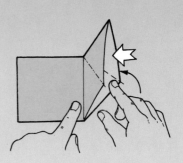

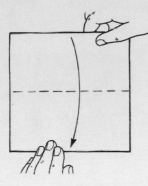

1 Fold the square in half from top to bottom, with the white side on top.

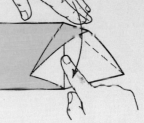

4 and with your free hand press it down...

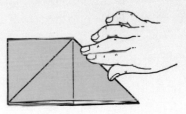

5 neatly into a triangle.

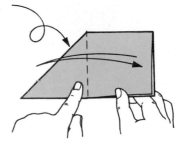

6 Turn the paper over. Repeat steps 2 to 5, so making a shape that in origami is called the waterbomb base.

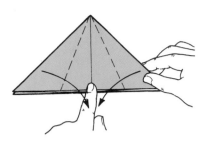

DRACULA'S FANGS

This model is ideal as a decoration on a piece of Halloween notepaper or stationery.

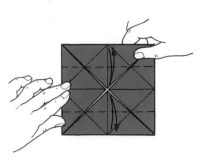

You will need:
Square of paper, coloured on one side and white on the other

7 From the top point, fold the topmost right- and left-hand sloping sides over to lie along the middle fold-line.

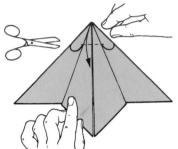

8 Carefully cut the paper as shown. Fold the top point down, so making the bat's head and ears appear.

1 With the white side on top, fold and unfold the square's opposite corners together to mark the diagonal fold-lines, then open up again.

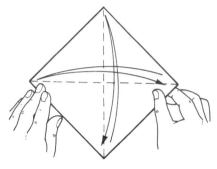

4 Fold the top and bottom edges in to meet the middle. Press them flat and unfold them.

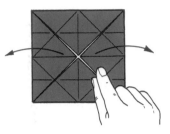

5 Unfold two middle corners as shown.

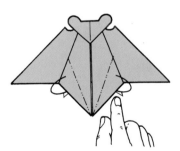

9 Fold the front flaps lower sloping edges behind, so making the bat's feet.

2 Fold the corners in to meet the middle, so making a shape that in origami is called the blintz base.

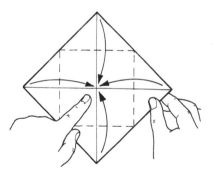

6 Fold the bottom edge in to meet the middle.

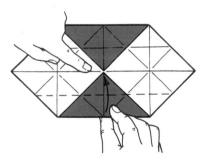

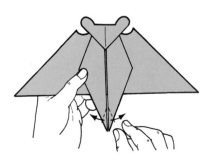
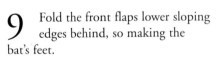

10 To complete the bat, fold the tips of its feet out to either side.

3 Once again, fold the corners in to meet the middle. Press them flat and unfold them.

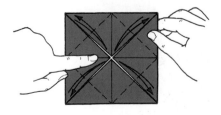

7 Along the existing fold-lines, inside reverse fold the lower right-hand section of paper as shown.

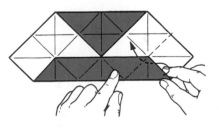

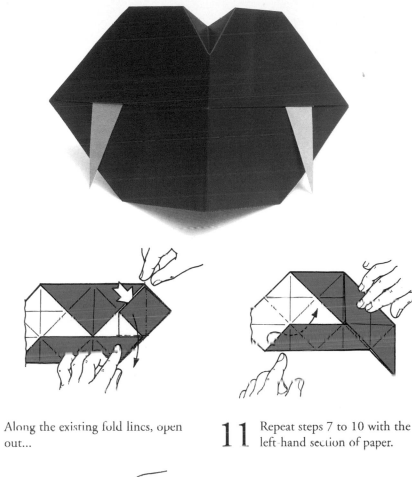

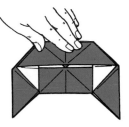

14 This should be the result. Press the paper flat.

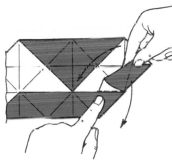

8 Along the existing fold lines, open out...

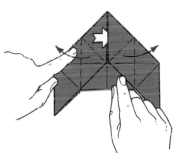

11 Repeat steps 7 to 10 with the left-hand section of paper.

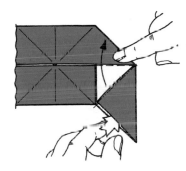

15 Lift up the right-hand pointed flap. Open it out and press it down neatly into a diamond.

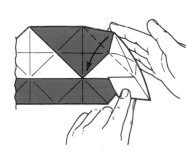

9 lift up and...

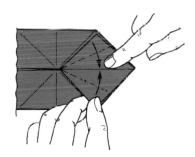

12 Along the existing fold-lines, open out the middle edges, so...

16 Fold the diamond's sloping edges in to meet the middle fold-line as shown.

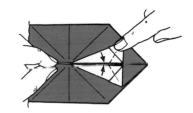

10 press down neatly the right-hand section of paper as shown, so making a pointed flap.

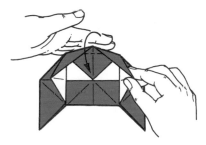

13 flattening down the top point.

17 Pinch together the diamond's sloping sides and...

25

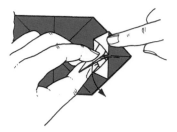

18 fold the pointed flap that appears down towards you. Press it flat, so making a fang.

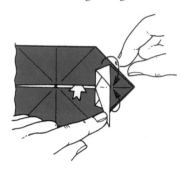

19 Tuck the fang's flaps...

20 inside the model. Press the paper flat.

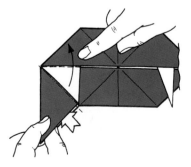

21 Repeat steps 15 to 20 with the left-hand pointed flap.

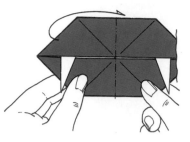

22 Fold one side point behind the other.

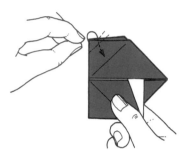

23 Push in a little of the top point.

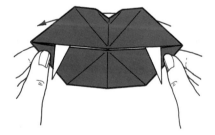

24 To complete Dracula's fangs, open them out into the position shown.

RAT

Try to get hold of the right kind of paper to match a rat's appearance, to enhance the finished result.

You will need:
Square of paper, coloured on one side and white on the other

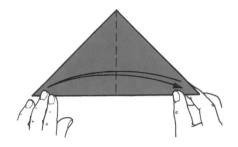

1 Repeat step 1 of the WIZARD'S HAT on page 4. Fold and unfold the diaper fold in half from side to side.

2 Fold the right- and left-hand halves of the bottom edge up to meet the middle fold-line.

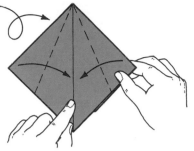

3 Fold the two top points down to meet the bottom point.

6 Turn the paper over from side to side. From the top point, fold the sloping sides in to meet the middle fold-line.

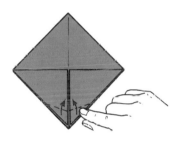

 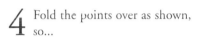

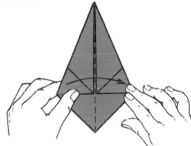

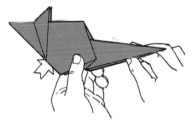

4 Fold the points over as shown, so...

7 Fold the paper in half from left to right.

10 Open the model out along the bottom edge.

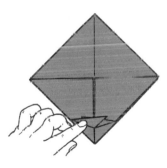

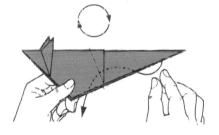

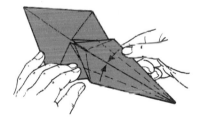

5 making the rat's ears.

8 Turn the paper around into the position shown. Inside reverse fold the right-hand point down inside the model.

11 Narrow down the tail as show

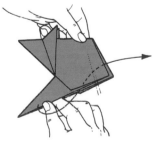

9 Inside reverse fold the point back out, so making the rat's tail.

12 Close the model up.

27

OWL

13 Fold the lower points up inside the model.

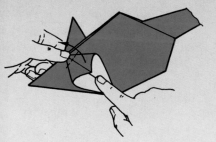

14 Open out an ear and press it down neatly into a diamond shape.

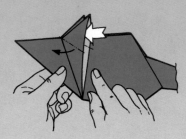

15 Open out the ear, so that it becomes three-dimensional. Repeat steps 14 and 15 with the remaining ear.

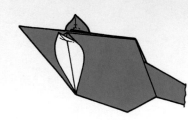

16 Here is the completed rat.

Try changing the angle of the eyes each time you make this model to see how many different expressions you can give your owl.

You will need:
2 squares of paper the same size, coloured on one side and white on the other
Glue

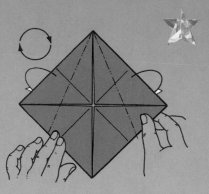

1 **Head:** Repeat steps 1 and 2 of DRACULA'S FANGS on page 24, with one square. Turn the blintz base around into the position shown. From the top point, fold the sloping sides behind, in to meet the middle fold-line.

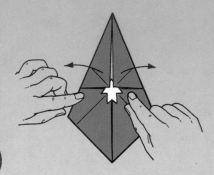

2 Unfold the two middle corners as shown.

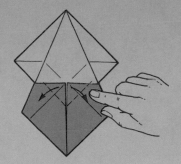

3 Fold the remaining middle corners out and...

7 Pinch together the triangle's sloping sides and...

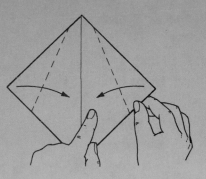

11 **Body:** Repeat step 1 of the BLOOD DROP on page 4, with the remaining square. Starting short of the top point, fold the sloping sides in towards the middle fold-line as shown.

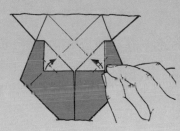

4 back in a little, so suggesting the owl's eyes.

8 fold the pointed flap that appears to one side.

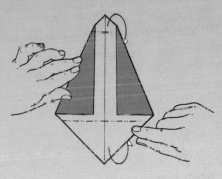

12 Fold the top and bottom points behind.

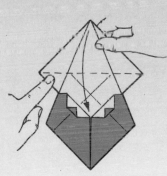

5 Fold the top points down on a line between the two side points as shown.

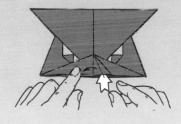

9 Open out the triangular flap and press it down neatly into a diamond.

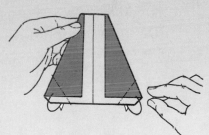

13 To complete the body, fold the lower edges behind.

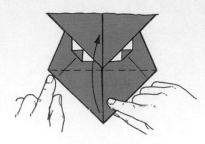

6 Fold the bottom point up on a line between the two side points as shown, so making a triangle.

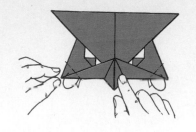

10 To complete the head, fold the bottom points behind.

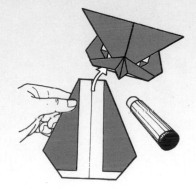

14 To complete the owl, glue the body inside the head at the desired angle.

FLYING WITCH

Stick this model to a window on a moonlit night. The witch will look as though she is flying past!

You will need:
3 squares of paper all the same size, coloured on one side and white on the other
Scissors
Glue

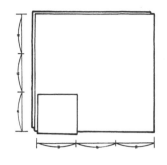

1 **Face:** From one square, cut out a square for the face to the size shown.

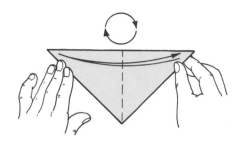

2 Repeat step 1 of the WIZARD'S HAT on page 4. Turn the diaper fold around as shown. Fold and unfold it in half from side to side.

3 Fold the left-hand point in to meet the middle.

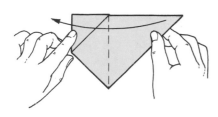

4 Along the existing fold-line, fold the right-hand point over to the left.

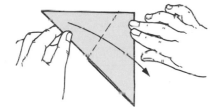

5 Fold the point over at an angle, so making the nose.

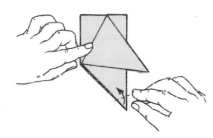

6 Fold a little of the bottom point over, so making the chin.

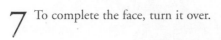

7 To complete the face, turn it over.

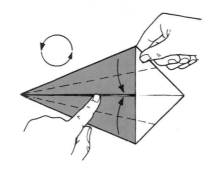

8 **Broomstick:** Repeat steps 1 and 2 of the BLOOD DROP on page 4 with another square. Turn the kite base around into the position shown. From the left-hand point, fold the sloping sides in to meet the middle fold-line.

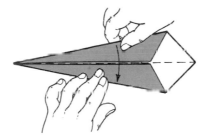

9 Fold the top down to the bottom.

10 Here is the completed broomstick.

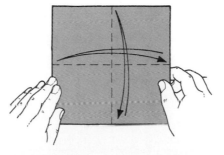

11 **Body:** Fold and unfold the remaining square in half from top to bottom and side to side, with the coloured side on top, then open up again.

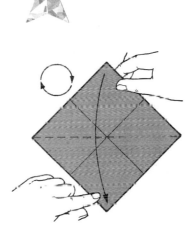

12 Turn the paper around to look like a diamond. Fold it in half from top to bottom, so making an upside down diaper fold.

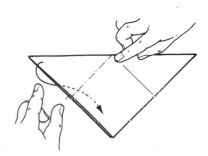

13 Along the existing fold-lines, inside reverse fold the top left-hand point, down...

14 inside the diaper fold.

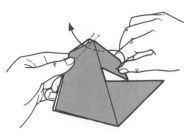

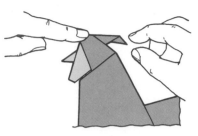

18 Inside reverse fold the point back up, so making the witch's hat.

22 This should be the result.

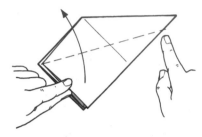

15 Fold the topmost layer of paper over as shown.

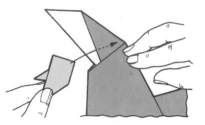

19 Glue the face inside the hat as shown.

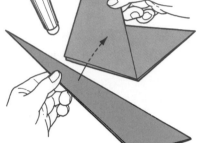

23 To complete the flying witch, glue the broomstick into place as shown.

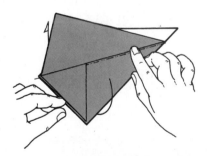

16 Repeat step 15 behind.

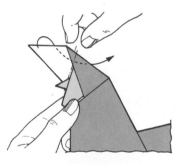

20 Inside reverse fold the hat's tip to the right.

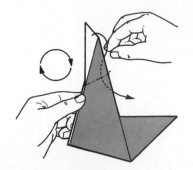

17 Turn the paper around into the position shown. Inside reverse fold the top point down as shown.

21 Fold the hat's top edge behind.